Moonmallow
Smoothie

First published 2003 by
A & C Black Publishers Ltd
37 Soho Square, London, W1D 3QZ

www.acblack.com

Text copyright © 2003 Philip Wooderson
Inside illustrations copyright © 2003 Martin Salisbury
Cover illustration copyright © 2003 Darren Lock

ISBN 0-7136-6571-8

A CIP catalogue for this book is available from the British Library.

A&C Black uses paper produced with elemental chlorine-free
pulp, harvested from managed sustained forests.

Printed and bound in Spain by G. Z. Printek, Bilbao.

PHILIP WOODERSON

Moonmallow Smoothie

Illustrated by
Martin Salisbury

A & C Black • London

To Tom, with love

Chapter One

BOING!

I dreamt that I took a big jump off a springboard into a pool.

THUMP!

I hit the bottom. The noise must have woken me up because I was wide awake when I heard the third noise.

SPLAT!

The ground vibrated, the bedroom window rattled and I leapt out of bed. I couldn't see out through the glass – it was covered in brown drippy stuff – so I hurried downstairs and out of the door, into our back garden.

The moon was shining brightly enough for me to see right to the bottom, where Dad had made a round pond. There was something in it, something big, looming up in the air. I needed a closer look. I squelched across the wet grass.

It was sizzling, steaming and pock-marked, like a mega-monster version of Mum's one and only attempt at making a Christmas pudding – except that Christmas puddings don't drop out of the sky (not even the smallest ones you get from the supermarket).

So was it a bomb? Was it going to explode?

Or was it a UFO?

Lights were going on now in windows in other houses, as Dad charged out of the back door, flashing his torch down the garden.

'Dad,' I called. 'What on Earth is it?'

He peered at it, holding one hand out as if to warm himself in front of a blazing bonfire. He shook his head in amazement.

'I'd say it's come millions of miles. It's burnt right down to the core and here it is now, in our garden – our very own meteorite!'

In minutes, the street was jammed with fire engines and ambulances.

But there was no fire to put out and nobody had been injured.

'Lucky for you,' said the Fire Chief. 'If that had come down on your house, sir, you wouldn't be standing here now!'

It must have whizzed through the sky, like a plane coming down to land. The Fire Chief said it had bounced off the metal roof of the local supermarket, and bounced off the bowling club green, destroying their well-kept lawn, before coming down one final time – SPLAT! – in our pond.

Lucky us!

At school the following morning, people

asked loads of questions, not just about where it had come from, but what would we do with it?

I said Dad wasn't too sure yet.

But when I got home, I found scientists examining it with gadgets.

'No need for concern,' they decided. 'We'll winch it out with a crane and take it away for some tests.'

'You won't.' Dad jutted his chin. 'I think this should be finders, keepers.'

'But you didn't find it—'

'*It* found *us*. So it's only fair that we keep it.'

Mum wasn't too pleased. 'I don't want it. It's only a vast lump of rock!'

'In that case,' Dad retorted, 'why did those government boffins want it to do lots of tests? I might want to do my own tests!'

'Oh wonderful!' Mum exploded. 'You haven't even got time to mend the hole in our roof!'

Dad ran his own ice cream parlour and made all the ice cream himself, but somehow, though he worked so hard, he never made any money.

'This might make our fortune,' said Dad. 'I've got to find out what's inside it!'

Mum guessed it might be full of ... rock.

But on the following Sunday Dad hired a pneumatic drill.

The drill made a terrible din. Dad drilled away for three hours. The garden got covered in dust. Neighbours phoned up to complain. But the noise only finally stopped when Dad hit a technical hitch.

'I've bored a deep hole!' Dad called out. 'But now the drill's got stuck.'

'If he's broken that drill,' said Mum, 'he'll have to pay for a new one! I'm sorry, I've had enough.'

The next time I saw Mum she was lugging a holdall out to the car.

'Where are you going?' I asked, with a terrible sinking feeling because this had happened before.

'You're coming as well,' said Mum.

'No way, not to Barry. He's boring.'

Uncle Barry lived near the golf course, with

his boring daughter, Zoe, who stayed in her room all the time listening to CDs by her favourite pop star, Michael Angelo.

'He can afford to be *boring*,' said Mum, shooting Dad a frightening glance. 'I'm talking about my brother who does an ordinary job and lives in an ordinary house that doesn't have holes in the roof or a huge rock in the garden.'

'Oh, that sort of *boring*!' said Dad, risking a smile at the drill.

Mum came and grabbed my arm. 'I'm not coming back while that rock's here. He'll have to get rid of it first.'

I thought this was really unfair. 'Dad can't get rid of the rock, Mum. Not till he's finished his tests.'

'Then he'll have to manage without us. Don't argue, just get in the car.'

Chapter Two

The next week was really boring. It wasn't until the next weekend that Mum let me go and see Dad.

As soon as Dad opened the door, I asked how the 'tests' were going.

'I'm on to something,' said Dad.

I knew, from what Mum had told me, the hire firm were on to him for wrecking their pneumatic drill. But from the keen look on his face I wondered if Dad had struck lucky?

He opened the fridge. It was empty, except for a small white cube, the size of a sugar lump, on one of Mum's best tea plates, covered over with cling film.

'Do you need to keep the rock fresh, Dad?' I asked.

'And dry,' said Dad. 'It's unstable. Now, take a good sniff.'

It smelt quite nice: like almonds and orange peel. I dabbed it with my finger and took a cautious lick. It tasted incredible – out of this world, but so strong it burnt my tongue and left it all fizzy and sticky.

Dad laughed. 'Let me show you something.'

Lifting the lump off the plate, Dad took it across to the sink and dropped it into the bowl. It sank, then seethed and frothed, heaving up out of the sink like freaky shaving foam, wobbling all over the place, shoving Mum's tea plate over the edge to smash on the kitchen floor. It spilled down the front of the cupboard. I stumbled back, horrified.

And meanwhile, the lump in the sink was still spouting heaps more foam – bubbling, popping and zizzing.

'I don't think I like this one bit, Dad!'

'Why not? It's a crucial test. Very impressive – and in any case—' Dad wiped his brow. 'Relax, it's run out of steam now. But what do we do with it, eh?'

'Perhaps we should clear it up, Dad.'

Together we filled nine bin bags and piled them outside the back door. Then we stood looking down the garden at the meteorite.

Dad took a deep breath. 'It's amazing. We've discovered a new type of foam.'

It wasn't the sort of foam for stuffing into pillows, or filling up holes in walls, or spreading all over the attic to keep the house warm in the winter – not in its natural state, because it was wet and sloppy. Though what would happen, I wondered, if it were dried or cooked?

'I did put a bit in the oven,' said Dad. 'It melted and stuck to the tin. I broke a knife trying to cut it. The tin had to go in the bin.'

'What if we froze it?' I said.

'I tried, in my lab,' said Dad. (He meant our garage.) 'I'll show you.'

The freezer was at the far end. Dad took out a carton of ... foam.

'I left it two days, but it wouldn't freeze hard, so' – he took out another carton – 'I mixed up a bit with ice cream. Now this won't freeze, either. Stays sloppy.'

It looked like the softest marshmallow, so light you could almost drink it.

'It's more like a smoothie,' I said.

'No, smoothies are made of fruit,' said Dad, turning it upside down so it plopped out into his hand, wobbling but holding its shape. 'Would people want ice cream smoothie? Correction – a meteorite smoothie?'

But I had a better idea. I could see it in bright flashing lights outside the ice cream parlour. 'Let's call it the Moonmallow Smoothie!'

Chapter Three

I had to wait two weeks before I saw Dad again. This meant another two weeks staying with Uncle Barry. But Dad phoned every evening so I thought I knew what he was up to. I knew he was making progress, perfecting the Moonmallow Smoothie. However, I hadn't a clue that he'd started selling the Smoothie in the ice cream parlour. So when he took me along there after school on Friday, I got a big surprise.

I saw this sign in the window …

> **Try Tony Tondi's New Special**
> *Jellybean*
> *Moonmallow Smoothie!*
> **as featured on TV!!!**

'Featured on TV, Dad?'

Dad's lips formed a lazy smile. 'Perfectly true. Tell you later. After you've had your first taste.'

He spooned some into a goblet. It was blobby and pale and smooth. It was like eating melted marshmallow. Then I swallowed a lumpy object that nearly made me choke.

'It's only a jellybean, Sam,' said Dad. 'They go

rather well, don't you think so?'

I looked round. The parlour was crowded, and every one of the customers was slurping up Moonmallow Smoothie. How had it got so popular, in such a short time?

Dad nodded. 'The TV people came round to do a feature on ice cream for *The Real Food Show* – and I gave them some Moonmallow Smoothie. They voted it ten out of ten. The queues have been here ever since. And what's more' – Dad leant forward, his eyes going beady and shrewd – 'I've had other ice cream makers phoning up and complaining that I've stolen their customers! They think it's unfair and want my recipe! And when I say "no" they get nasty.

I even had Bernie Karbunkle, the ice cream millionaire, coming here, making an offer!'

'Incredible! What did you say, Dad?'

'That BK Products are absolute total garbage. "So no thanks, Bernie," I told him.'

'He can't have liked that.'

'Why should I care?'

Dad sounded so chirpy I laughed too. But the laugh didn't last. I was starting to say, 'It might have paid enough to get the roof mended at home, Dad—' But before I could get round to adding a bit about Mum coming home, a little girl at the next table spat out a jellybean.

'YaaaaaaaaaaaahhH!!!!!'

Her mother goggled. 'How dare you!'

'It's an egg with an insect in – *hatching*!'

'Rubbish!' Her mum stared at it. 'Hold on, though – it's got little legs!'

Dad jumped up and swabbed it away. 'Only a tiny bug, Ma'am. It must have buzzed in off the street.'

'But, please—' A little old lady was struggling to get to her feet. 'I'm sorry, I've got one too.'

She held it up on a spoon, but a man with a prickly moustache snatched it and peered at it crossly through shiny rimless glasses. 'Outrageous. This is a *cockroach*!'

'Oh, mind you own business,' Dad told him.

'It *is* my business,' the man snapped back.

'Because I'm a *health inspector*!'

The wretched health inspector made all the customers leave, then spent two hours in the kitchen, opening every cupboard, pulling out every drawer. Then he said the ice cream parlour shouldn't open again until he had time to come back and make a more thorough inspection.

'But listen—' Dad blurted. 'I make it at home, and I've never seen a cockroach in my garage. Have you, Sam?'

'Garage?' the health inspector echoed with keen disbelief.

'Laboratory,' I corrected.

The Inspector took out a pen. 'I'm serving a notice on you, sir,' he said, with his eyes fixed on Dad. 'Banning the use of your house, laboratory – or, indeed, garage – for the preparation of ice creams for sale to the general public.'

Chapter Four

I didn't sleep well that night. I felt so sorry for Dad. Next morning we stayed at home. The ice cream parlour was closed and Dad had nothing to do.

Taking a football outside, I kicked it against the wall, until our neighbour popped up: a wizened old man with fierce eyes, who was clutching a large pair of shears.

'Oh hi, Mr Bates,' I said.

Mr Stomper Bates had protested at all the dust and noise made by Dad's drilling attempt. But he was friendly enough. He was a retired policeman. His hobbies were gardening by day and playing the trumpet at night, and every Christmas he organised a pantomime in the school hall, with help from his old friend, Trundler (another retired policeman), who played the pantomime dame.

'I saw your Dad on the telly, on *The Real Food Show*,' growled Stomper. 'He's invented a new sort of ice cream that's not an ice cream, is that right?'

I grinned, full of pleasure and pride – until I remembered Dad's problems, and the grin faded into a frown.

Stomper noticed. 'What is it, young feller?'

But while I was explaining how those jellybeans must have been sabotaged by someone who harboured a grudge – like one of Dad's jealous rivals in the ice cream trade – Dad called out from the kitchen, 'Good news! I've just had a phone call!'

'Not from Mr Karbunkle?' I asked.

'No, from a hotel – in the city.'

The manager wanted to order enough Moonmallow Smoothie to serve to sixty guests, for a party next weekend.

'And one of the guests is world-famous, so there will be photographers, too. We might even get on the news!'

'But, Dad,' – I had to say this – 'where are you going to make it – I mean, without breaking the law?'

Dad carried on grinning. 'No problem. The manager – lovely lady – said we could use their kitchen at the Fright Hotel!'

'The Fright Hotel?' cried Stomper. 'I remember that place. The owner met a nasty end, so the hotel had to close down. I wonder who's bought it now?'

'The manager is called Audrey Bapp. And the funny thing is,' Dad chuckled, 'she wants the Moonmallow Smoothie shaped like a poodle.'

'What for, Dad?'

'To please her famous guest.'

'But how are we going to do that?'

Dad said it would be very easy. Audrey Bapp was providing a mould, plus any equipment Dad needed, and even a chauffeur-driven car to take us to the hotel.

'But what did you mean,' Dad asked Stomper, 'about the previous owner meeting a nasty end?'

Stomper looked a bit bashful. 'Fell into the ice cream churn, poor chap. Got frozen to death in ice cream!'

Chapter Five

Another boring week went by before I saw Dad again. He was outside school the following Friday. We went to the supermarket and filled up two large trolleys with sugar, eggs and cream to make enough Smoothie for sixty.

'Are you going to risk using jellybeans, Dad?'

'Not in a poodle, Sam,' said Dad. 'Except perhaps two – for its eyes.'

'Do you know who the famous guest is yet?'

He shook his head. 'Haven't a clue.'

Of course, I kept on wondering, but didn't have any idea until the following lunchtime, when we were watching TV, and there was a piece on the local news about Zoe's favourite pop star. Michael Angelo had arrived by plane, to perform in our city tonight! And there he was, at the airport, surrounded by screaming fans, with cameramen and reporters shouting questions at him.

Michael Angelo looked really shy, especially when one of them asked him, 'What are your favourite things?'

He stopped to think, and then replied, in such

a quiet voice it was hard to hear, 'I like writing songs. I like ice cream ... but best of all? My two poodles!'

Dad and I swapped glances. We both had the same thought at once. But before we could share our opinions the doorbell chimed and Dad jumped to his feet.

'Come on, it's the hotel car, they've come to collect us, Sam!'

Outside it was windy and wet. The sky was churning with clouds.

The hotel car was enormous, with soft leather seats and a chauffeur wearing a uniform.

As we moved off down the street, Stomper rushed out of his house, flapping his arms and shouting, as if he had something to tell us.

'He's just wishing us luck,' said Dad.

* * *

Although the Fright Hotel was near the city centre, it stood in its own private grounds behind some tall brick walls. The journey took twenty minutes. After drawing up at a grand entrance with pillars on either side, the chauffeur opened the doors for us and porters in uniforms hurried to unload our shopping.

The foyer was dimly lit by lamps with heavy, dark shades. To the left was a long, curved desk with an old-fashioned telephone. Behind it was a tall black dresser, with hooks for the keys to the rooms. Doors led to the Banqueting Suite, the Sunset Lounge and the ballroom. At the far end was a staircase curving up to a first-floor landing.

'Heeeeelllllloooooo?'

A bulky lady leant over the banister rails. She raised a hand – 'Hold your horses!' – then took the stairs two at a time. At the bottom she strode towards us.

'That's Audrey Bapp,' whispered Dad.

Her face was round like a doughnut, but dusted with powder not sugar. She wore spiky glasses with sparkly frames and a mauve scarf gleaming with sequins, but the rest of her clothing was plain. In her white housecoat and black woolly tights, she looked like a dinner lady dressed up for the school Christmas party.

'Who have we here?' she said, pointing at me. 'This cute little boy's not your helper?'

'My son,' said Dad.

'But I'm not "cute",' I said.

She tried to pinch my cheek but her hand was too big and too clumsy. I couldn't see why Dad liked her, except she had got him this job.

She took his arm. 'Follow me. I want to show you the ballroom where the party will be.'

I followed. The ballroom was enormous. Barry's house could have fitted inside it. The ceiling was like a blue sky, with giant glass chandeliers.

'We'll be having a buffet,' said Audrey, waving

a hand at the tables at the far end of the room. 'Nibbly things on the left and glasses and drinks on the right, leaving the middle table free for your Moonmallow Smoothie. But no time to waste,' she added briskly. 'Tonight's going to be a Big Night. I'll show you where you'll be working. Down in the cellars. Come on.'

Dad cleared his throat. 'Not the kitchens?'

'No, far too hot, and too busy, and Mooton, the Chef, might get jealous. He thinks he should make our ice cream!'

She turned to me. 'Aren't you proud, having a dad who can conjure up a brand new type of ice cream? And what a name: Moonmallow Smoothie! It just rolls off the tongue. What gave him the clever idea?'

'The mete—' I began, breaking off in mid-word as Dad poked me hard in the ribs.

'Meat?' Audrey said. 'In an ice cream?'

'No, just a trade secret,' said Dad.

'Hmmmm.' With a glint in her eye Audrey went on to say how she'd read in the local paper that 'one' had come down in our garden. 'A meteorite, that is. But what would that have to do with—?'

'Your "famous guest"?' Dad suggested. 'You've not told us who he is yet, but we've got a good idea. Haven't we, Sam?'

'Yes,' I cried. 'It's Michael Ange—'

'SSSSHHH!' went Audrey, opening a tiny door that I hadn't noticed before, and clattering off down some very steep stairs, leaving us both to follow.

The kitchen was crowded and noisy, with cooks in food-splattered overalls, stirring steamy cauldrons and rolling out sheets of pastry.

'They're feeling the strain,' Audrey told us, shouting to make herself heard. 'So many months with the place closed down and nothing to cook – not a sausage – then suddenly, action-stations. And there's my Head Chef, Monsieur Mooton, but try not to draw his attention.'

A little man with a very big paunch was chopping up tiny mushrooms with a gigantic knife.

'Why shouldn't he see us?' I asked.

'Because he's the chef,' said Audrey. 'He thinks he should make the ice cream.'

CRASH!

Everybody jerked round.

A cook with a pink, pimply face was looking down at a chocolate cake that was upside down on the floor.

'Awww-whoops – slipped out of my hands.'

Audrey pushed us towards the far doorway, before swinging round, rushing at him, shouting. 'You clumsy oaf, clear it up, bake a new one! I've got to have cake with the poodle!'

'What poodle?' said Mooton suspiciously.

'That's none of your business, just do it!'

And with that, she quickly joined us again, and guided us to the end of a very dark, gloomy passage with doors on either side, each one with a tiny window blocked with an iron grille. It was as if we were down in a prison. She unlocked the last door on the left.

The ice cream chamber was chilly. It had curving walls like an igloo – and cold stone tiles on the floor. On the right were shelves crammed with dishes and racks of whisks and spoons, as well as a deep china sink with a wooden draining board. On the left was a scrubbed wooden table, with all our shopping stacked on it and …

'Goodness, what's this?' exclaimed Dad.

I thought he meant the pink plastic mould shaped like a giant poodle. But he was pointing at something further back, in the far corner: a massive great iron contraption, shaped like a drum, with a lid on, crouching on curvy legs. A metal disc on its side said …

Hanson's
Original Patented
Electrical Ice Cream Churn

'Try not to fall in,' said Audrey. 'And as for you,' – she turned to me – 'come up and see me later. I've got a nice little job you can do that will help your dad.'

'Doing what?' I said.

'Making our famous guest feel at home. He's already here, you know, Sam!'

And with that she turned on her heels, leaving Dad and me alone in the ice cream chamber.

Chapter Six

I did my best to help: weighing kilograms of sugar and cracking a hundred eggs, separating the yolks for Dad to mix up with the cream. He whisked the lot in a bucket, then poured it into a big copper pan. While this was being heated slowly on the stove, I had to keep on stirring until it began to thicken into a nice rich custard.

(That's how you make *real* ice cream.)

Then Dad dropped a cube of the concentrate from the meteorite into a large bowl of water. It fizzled and frothed. It foamed out of the bowl like a massive great indoor firework.

'I think you've used too much, Dad.'

Dad stood back. 'Just relax, Sam.'

He had to let the custard cool before he could mix it up with the foam from the concentrate. 'Why don't you go and see Audrey?'

I wasn't keen to see Audrey again, but I thought of her 'famous guest'. There was nothing for me to do down here, so I set off, back up the passage.

I peered in through the other doorways.

There wasn't much to see, only a few old barrels, dusty bottles and cardboard boxes – until the last door on the left. This one was standing half-open. A lantern was perched on a crate, casting an eerie light.

I might have taken a closer look, except that the kitchen door opened, further along the passage, and out came one of the cooks. And I saw something really disgusting.

The cook fished out the chocolate cake. It came out in several lumps, studded with squashed green peas, but he put it all on a plate and stuck it together again. He carried it into the kitchen, presenting it to the Head Chef.

The other cooks watched in silence as Mooton inspected it carefully.

He poked at the peas with his finger, shaking his head, frowning sternly. 'Not good enough. It needs *more* peas!'

The cooks gave a rousing cheer, and as they formed a circle, as if to dance around it, Mooton held up the cake, announcing in his French accent, 'Deees way we weell get our revenge upon dat 'orrible lady for bringing dat 'orrible "ice cream man" to work in our 'otel, eh, boys?'

'That's it, that's it!' they all bellowed.

I scooted across the kitchen and sprinted away up the stairs.

In the ballroom, I was so shaky I hardly

noticed the waiters helping themselves from the buffet. I headed towards the foyer.

The foyer was crowded with guests, checking in, getting their keys. The porters were lugging in baggage. I asked one where to find Audrey. He pointed upstairs. 'In her office!'

Up on the first floor landing, I set off along a wide corridor with a deep red, patterned carpet. But halfway along it, I stopped. I could hear a peculiar noise. A yowling sound. Then a bark. Then a maid came out of an open door, wheeling a cleaning trolley.

But before I could ask if she happened to know where the manager's office might be, another door opened, further along, and a man in a suit stepped out.

'Room service? We need some ice cream!'

'I'm just changing towels,' said the maid.

'My boss don't need towels, he wants Smoothie – for soothing his vocal chords, so he can *sing* tonight!'

I took a deep breath. 'Is your boss called—?'

'*Sssshhhhh*—' said a voice, close behind me.

I spun round and Audrey grabbed my wrist with her big clumsy hand. 'Come with me!'

We went up more flights of stairs.

Up on the top, fifth floor, the boards were bare and splintered, and the walls were a muddy green. Overhead was a murky skylight shrouded in dirty cobwebs, casting a dingy glow. Audrey tugged me into a drab little room with a fold-out bed, crooked chairs and a cheap little dressing table, loaded with tubes of make-up.

She made me sit down, then she told me, leaning over me so I could see her teeth: pearly white, flecked with tiny red specks from her red lipsticked lips.

'The thing is, I need your help, Sam.' She gave me a long searching look. 'You've guessed who our famous guest is. But the fact is that Michael is shy.'

I stared at her, saying nothing.

'That means he's quite likely to try and slip out without even meeting our guests. But if he misses the party, he won't get to try your dad's ice cream, and you don't want that, do you, Sam?'

I shook my head.

'Good, nor do I. So what I want you to do is go and ask him nicely if he'd like to taste the Smoothie down in the ice cream chamber. In private, without being hassled. That way he'll meet your dad, Sam, and afterwards I'll make sure there's a photographer ready to take a few snaps of Michael along with your dad and the Smoothie. Clickitty-click. How's that sound, eh? You do want your dad in the papers?'

I wanted the pop star to like Dad's ice cream. I wanted Mum to find out, so she'd be proud and come home again soon.

'You bet!' I said.

'That's the spirit.' She gave me a pat on the head.

Chapter Seven

One good turn deserved another, I thought. If Audrey was helping Dad like this, the least I could do was tell her about that choc-'n'-pea cake.

I did, but she didn't believe me.

'Only a joke, Sam, don't worry. They'll have chucked the cake back in the bin.'

I wasn't so sure.

'Don't believe me? OK, Sam, you check at the buffet.'

* * *

By the time Audrey was ready to take me down to the ballroom, the party was in full swing, with crowds of red-faced grown-ups all eating, drinking and laughing. The wine had made everyone noisy.

I overheard two old men.

'So who's gonna be the next mayor, eh? I'm voting for Bernie Karbunkle!'

They went on. 'Such a nice fellow!'

'Helping Freddy Fright's widow to get this place re-opened!'

'And letting the manager, Audrey Bapp, hire another ice cream man to make the ice cream for the party—'

'—must have felt sorry for Tondi having his parlour closed down.'

'But Bernie's not here at the party?'

'Nah. Out of the country. On business.'

I finally got to the buffet. No sign of the chocolate cake. But before I could stock up with something to eat, Audrey was tugging my arm.

'Mike's concert begins in an hour, Sam. They've sent two limos to fetch him. There's one outside the front entrance and another one round the back.'

'What for?'

'So he can slip away without being seen by his fans, or saying hello at the party.'

'Because he's so shy?'

'Yes, exactly. But he's got to try the ice cream, Sam, and now is the time so – go for it!'

I hurried back up the stairs. Two men in black suits blocked the corridor outside the pop star's suite. Then out came Michael Angelo, wearing a lime green suit.

How Zoe would envy me now, meeting her favourite pop star!

But before I could even say 'Smoothie!' his two poodles bounded out.

They were monsters, as big as Alsatians. They reared up, knocking me backwards, shoving their tongues in my face.

'Get off, Moll and Poll!' shouted Michael.

The minders in suits grabbed their leashes.

'What do you want?' asked Michael, helping me back on my feet.

This gave me my chance, so I told him: Dad was down in the basement, waiting to give him a taste of Moonmallow Smoothie, in private.

'Too late, there's no time,' snapped a minder. 'It's only an hour till the concert!'

'The concert can wait,' said the pop star. 'My vocal chords need their ice cream!'

* * *

The minders followed us down, tugging the poodles behind them, passing the door to the ballroom. They ended up down in the kitchen.

'But where's the ice cream?' cried Michael.

'Not here,' I said. 'Keep your voice down.'

Too late. Mooton blocked our path.

'No ice cream in 'ere!' said the Head Chef. 'And no dogs allowed in my kitchens.'

I noticed that massive great knife in his hand.

'Not ice cream,' I murmured. 'Just Smoothie.'

Surprised, Mooton lowered the knife, and before he could raise it again, I dragged Michael past the cooks, leading him down the passage towards the ice cream chamber. The cooks all followed, protesting.

I opened the door. Dad turned round in surprise.

'Here's Michael Angelo, Dad!'

Dad smiled at me in triumph!

His Smoothie was wobbly but perfectly shaped, like a giant snow-white poodle (with two jelly beans for eyes), squatting on a brown base of chocolatey—

Dad had been tricked!

Mooton must have given Dad the sabotaged cake to go under the Moonmallow Smoothie. But before I had time to warn Dad, Michael was in the chamber and Dad slammed the door in my face, to hold all those cooks at bay. The cooks were jeering and laughing now. They'd seen the chocolate base too!

I called out, banged on the door, but no good, the grille was tight shut.

There was only one thing I could do: run back up the stairs and warn Audrey!

* * *

The guests in the ballroom were lining up to have their photographs taken. Audrey was in the middle, her voice booming loud and clear over the general hubbub.

'It's thanks to Mr Karbunkle we're having this party tonight. He's asked me to tell you how sorry he is he can't be with us in person.'

'Where's Michael Angelo?' somebody called.

'He might drop in any moment, before he goes off to his concert or—'

Audrey suddenly saw me. 'Sam?'

There was deathly silence, with everyone staring and listening.

Reporters were holding their mikes up, photographers were raising their cameras. But before I could push any closer – to whisper into her ear about those squashy peas in the cake under Dad's Moonmallow Smoothie – the minders burst into the room, trying to rein back the poodles.

More noise and excitement, loud cheering, the guests calling, 'Is he coming? Michael Angelo's here – where is he?'

The poodles plunged towards Audrey.

'We've lost him!' cried the first minder.

The second one shouted, 'He's … *vanished*!'

Chapter Eight

'Pop stars *don't* vanish,' said Audrey. 'If Mr Angelo's not here, it's because he's still somewhere else.'

'But where? Where? *Where?*' cried the guests.

'He was down with Tondi – Sam's dad,' said Audrey.

'But not any more!' cried a minder. 'We looked in that ice cream chamber. Tondi's not there either – not now!'

The poodles yowled in distress.

'Well, don't just stand there,' cried Audrey. 'Let's search the hotel, top to bottom!!!'

We all poured down through the kitchens. We searched every one of those cellars. Then everyone – guests, cooks, cameramen – went barging back up the stairs. We poured through the Sunset Lounge, burst into the Banqueting Suite, turned over the billiard room and ransacked the Sunset Lounge.

We all jogged round the gym, steamed our way through the sauna, swarmed round the swimming pool and charged through the changing rooms, opening all the lockers, and looking in all the loos.

Then we moved up to the bedrooms, going through every wardrobe, checking beneath every bed, peering behind all the curtains. But no luck. Back in the foyer, we came to rest, shaking our heads.

Audrey reached for the phone. 'I don't think the police will believe this …'

But as she was dialling their number, the entrance doors started revolving, letting in six policemen, followed by a grim man in a damp brown overcoat who flashed an ID wallet.

'Is Mr Angelo here, please?'

'He … was,' said Audrey, softly.

'His limo's still waiting outside,' said the cop.

'And all his fans,' agreed Audrey. 'But how did *you* get here so quickly?'

The plain-clothes detective looked around at all our anxious faces. 'The fact is, we've just got a message from a so-called "Ice Cream Man". He claims that he's got Michael Angelo, and he's going to hold him hostage – until he receives a ransom for rather a large sum of money.'

I stepped back, feeling dizzy.

'I don't believe this,' cried Audrey, her hands going up to her face. 'You don't mean to say that Sam's father—?'

'Dad hasn't—' I stammered. 'Dad can't have—'

The policemen were glaring at me.

'That boy helped his dad,' said a
lured Michael down the back stairs,
ice cream!'

'Is that so?' The detective pulled
handcuffs. 'In that case – he's under a1   ...

I bolted. I dashed for the exit.

I pushed the revolving glass door. I thought
it was going to be heavy. Instead it spun round
so fast it sent me shooting out, whamming me
hard from behind. I went tumbling down the
steps. I sprawled on the bright red carpet laid
down specially for Michael, and stumbled back
on to my feet as the first of the six policemen
came tumbling out behind me.

'Stop! Stop!' he ordered.

No way!

I was off down the drive, sprinting as fast as I
could.

The main gate was closed and guarded.
Security men faced the crowds. There must
have been thousands of girls, all making so
much noise nobody heard the policemen still
shouting and chasing behind me.

But suddenly, out of nowhere, a hand
reached out and grabbed me, spinning me
round, off the driveway, tugging me into the
bushes.

I opened my mouth to scream but a hand
clamped over my lips.

Chapter Nine

The six policemen charged past. And then I was being pushed from behind down a path, round behind the hotel. We came out in a cobbled yard.

It was dark, lit only by one feeble lamp over a shuttered door, next to a huge iron skip heaped full of garbage bags.

A man stepped out from its shadow. He was fat, with whisps of white hair bushing from under his cap. 'Who goes there?'

From behind I heard, 'Me, you twerp.'

'Oh, yes. Who's with you, Stomper?'

Stomper? I turned round to face him, overwhelmed by enormous relief.

'I thought you were a policeman – a *real* policeman!' I gasped.

'I was, don't you remember? So was old Trundler,' said Stomper.

'And uniforms *do* come in useful. We merged with the ranks,' said Trundler.

'Thank goodness,' I blurted. 'But why are you here?'

Stomper and Trundler swapped glances. And then I remembered Stomper rushing out of his gate, as the chauffeur drove us away. 'How did you guess there would be trouble?'

'We didn't,' Stomper admitted.

'We just saw the news,' said Trundler.

'What news?'

'At lunchtime, of course. The bit about Michael Angelo loving ice cream and his poodles. We twigged it. We had to be here.'

'But why?'

Stomper sniffed and snorted as Trundler owned up to the fact they both liked Michael's music so much. 'We wanted his autograph, Sam.'

'Now tell us the worst,' broke in Stomper. 'Come on, Sam. What's been happening?'

'Michael Angelo's vanished,' I said. 'And everyone's blaming Dad.'

The two old men gawped in horror.

I gave them a few more details.

'But I've been on guard here,' said Trundler, 'in case he went out this way, and Stomper was out at the front. So who saw him leave? Wasn't us.'

'The hotel was searched, top to bottom. Except for the roof,' I admitted.

'You think he'd have jumped? Can he fly?'

'Now don't be daft, Trundler!' said Stomper. 'I bet they got out through the cellars.'

'Except there aren't any windows or outside doors,' I said. 'Although,' – I thought of something – 'while Dad was making the ice cream, I wandered along the passage and looked in one of the cells, and someone was there – with a lantern.'

'To give 'em some light?' wondered Stomper.

'But there were electric lights, too.'

'So?'

'So why bring a lantern, unless you were going somewhere that didn't have proper electric lights?'

'Like, what are you hinting at, Sammy?'

I gave a slight shrug. 'It's just an idea, but you don't think there's some sort of passage? Like an underground, secret passage, that might lead out of the cellars?'

Stomper humphed. 'I very much doubt it.'

'I wonder ...' Trundler gazed at me, and even in the darkness I saw his eyes were twinkling. 'One has to consider these things.'

'How long will that take?' Stomper wondered.

'You want to go home, do you, Stomper?'

'If only we could,' I agreed.

'We can. Come with us,' said Trundler. 'We're in The Uniform, aren't we?'

* * *

So round we went to the front gate.

The fans were still waiting for Michael. Rumours were spinning, that one of the giant poodles had bitten the pop star so badly the concert might have to be cancelled.

Stomper walked up to the guards. 'Evening, all.'

A guard waved us through. 'Caught the boy, then?'

'We're taking him down to the station.'

A cab driver opened his rear door. 'How come you aren't using a squad car?'

'Cutbacks,' said Stomper. 'Get going.'

The streets were choked with fans still hoping to glimpse their hero.

The drive took more than an hour. As the cab turned into our street, I caught sight of three police vans parked outside our house. Lights blazed from all the windows.

'I can't go in there,' I protested.

'Come into our house,' said Stomper. 'Act natural, they won't even see you.'

And luckily nobody did.

* * *

Bolting the door behind us, Trundler whistled a tune.

'Relax, relax, we're quite safe now!'

But I was far too tense, thinking of all those detectives rummaging round my house. And when I looked out of the window I saw more police in the garden, flashing torches about.

Trundler patted my shoulder. 'Hot chocolate?'

A coal fire glowed in the grate, casting warm reflections over the red-painted walls. Old photographs in silver frames showed Stomper blowing his trumpet, and Trundler wearing a bonnet, dressed up as a pantomime dame.

I sat on the edge of a comfy armchair. 'I wish I could just work it out. Who'd kidnap Michael Angelo? It's someone who wants the money. But why should they try and blame Dad, unless …'

I began to wonder. I thought of those sabotaged jellybeans, and the health inspector on hand to get Dad's parlour closed down. 'Someone's out to get him – but who?'

Stomper took off his cap and spun it like a

frisbee on to the living room table. 'I'm fuddled.'

'Be-fuddled,' said Trundler, settling down on the sofa. 'Be-wildered. Be seated, Stomper.'

'By now the police might have found some more clues,' I said, not feeling too hopeful.

As if to answer my question, Stomper switched on the TV news.

'We go live to our reporter outside the Fright Hotel. Judith, what is the latest?'

'There's no doubt now,' said Judith, wearing an anorak lined with fake fur. 'Michael Angelo *has* been kidnapped. I'm here with the City Police Chief ...'

'Uh yeah ...' said the City Police Chief. 'We don't have a clue how the gang got away, though we're certain they did. It's a mystery!'

Then Audrey appeared – on the telly!

'We're all so worried for Michael ...' Audrey had tears in her eyes. 'And naturally I feel it's *my* fault – for hiring that evil man to make the ice cream.'

It took a moment for this to sink in – that she meant my dad. 'He's not *evil*! How could she say such a thing? She can't really think that Dad's guilty!'

Stomper switched off the telly. 'Nasty old cow,' he said flatly.

'Reminds me of someone,' said Trundler. 'Out of my distant past ...'

'Something else to reflect on,' said Stomper. 'I mean, if you've finished reflecting on ... what was it before ... secret passages?'

Trundler looked peeved. Then his face lit up. 'That's it. I've finally got it.'

'Got what?'

'The answer you crave, Stomp. The mystery's solved. It's the – sewer!'

'Come again?'

Trundler beamed. 'People tend to forget but sewers go under buildings, and big buildings need big sewers.'

'You mean,' growled Stomper, 'you're *hinting*, this kidnap gang might have got away via an underground waste-pipe?'

'Why not? We should check!' I demanded.

'You mean with the Council?' said Trundler, sounding a little uncertain. 'But they won't be open till Monday.'

'Too late. What else can we do? D'you think there's a website?' I asked.

'Let's have a look now,' said Stomper.

Stomper kept his computer under an old tartan blanket, on a small desk in the corner. It took a few minutes to log on. He was using his old police ID, and strangely it still did the trick to access the website he needed.

He checked though Public Records and soon had a diagram on the screen with thin green lines like branches, sprouting from fat red lines.

'I'm staggered,' said Stomper. 'You're spot on. One of the main sewage tunnels goes under the Fright Hotel!'

'So that's how they did it,' said Trundler, pointing a podgy finger at a red blob on the line. 'Whoever "they" are. I bet you they came up for fresh air by way of that manhole there. Into a nice quiet back street where their getaway car picked 'em up!'

'Except you've missed something, Trundler.'

'And what might that be, my dear Stomper?'

'How "they" got in the sewer, from the hotel, because' – Stomper drew himself upright – 'according to what's on this screen here, there isn't a single manhole under the Fright Hotel. The nearest is outside the back gate, and we know the back gate was padlocked!'

'So they had to dig their own manhole, to burrow up into the cellar.' Trundler beamed at him broadly. 'But don't take my word for it, Stomper. Much better to check for yourself.'

'You want me to go down a sewer?'

'Well, *I* would.'

'Why don't you?' snapped Stomper.

'Because I'm too broad in the beam, Stomp.'

'I'll come with you, Stomper,' I offered. 'It's our only hope to trace Dad. I mean, whoever these kidnappers are, they've kidnapped Dad too. He's with them.'

'That's true,' Trundler said. 'For the moment. At least till the ransom's been paid.'

Stomper hunched his shoulders. 'But then what?'

I did my own thinking out loud. 'If a gang is trying to use my dad, pretending he's their leader, they'll never dare release him because he'll know who they are!'

'So what are you saying?' growled Stomper.

'That we've got to rescue him, Stomper. So we'll have to go down that sewer.'

'They won't still be down there,' said Stomper.

'But they'll have left footprints,' said Trundler. 'You'd just have to follow them, see where they go to!'

Stomper kept rubbing his chin. 'It's too late tonight.'

'In the morning?'

'First thing would be best,' said Trundler.

Chapter Ten

After making these plans for the morning, Stomper said it was time to sleep. He lent me a pair of pyjamas four or five sizes too big and led me up to the spare bedroom.

But I was too wound up to sleep.

Instead, I kept thinking of Dad, wondering where he might be, hoping he was OK. I shuffled across to the window and peered out into the night. No one was out in our garden now. I guessed the police must have gone. The sky was a sour shade of orange from all the sodium lamps fizzling on empty streets across the sleeping city. It was dreadful to think, somewhere out there, somewhere not far away, Dad might be locked in a room like this, looking out into the night, hoping and praying for rescue.

I could hear Stomper and Trundler snoring away in their bedrooms. How could they be sleeping already? I felt completely alone.

The moon came out from behind a tall cloud, and our garden was dusted with moonshine. Pulling the window open, I breathed in the damp chilly air. I put my own clothes back on.

It wasn't a difficult jump on to the garden wall. It wasn't too hard to scramble down on to the patio outside our back door. A spare key was under the flowerpot. I let myself into the kitchen.

There were still dirty plates in the sink, left over from lunch – a few hours back. It seemed such a long time ago.

Upstairs, I checked my bedroom.

The police had left fingerprint powder all over my chest of drawers, and knocked over one of my best model planes, snapping its propeller.

I hadn't really come back home for any particular reason, but when I caught sight of my own comfy bed I suddenly felt so tired I knew what I needed to do. Worming down under the duvet, I closed my eyes for a bit.

I must have slept for a while, though when I opened my eyes it was still dark outside. I looked out of my bedroom window.

The moon lit up the crater where Dad's pond had once been. But there was something missing.

The meteorite! Where had it gone?

A meteorite couldn't vanish – any more than a famous pop star.

Yet when I rushed outside and ran down the garden path I couldn't detect any scuff-marks, broken branches or flattened grass. Only the empty hole.

The sky flickered white for an instant. I heard a faint rumble of thunder. Then I noticed a small plastic signboard, stuck on a stick nearby ...

CONFISCATION NOTICE
THE COST FOR REMOVAL OF OBJECT TO BE MET BY OWNER OF THE LAND.
BY ORDER
- HEALTH INSPECTOR -

* * *

Stomper was up by now, in his kitchen, wearing baggy camouflage trousers and a cap on his stubbly head. He was loading a rucksack with ropes.

'I've made us some sandwiches, Sam. I hope you like cheese and pickle.'

'Well, I do,' said Trundler. 'I love 'em. And I've been busy as well. I've printed a map of the sewers for Sam, in case old Stomper falls in and gets swept away in the sewage.'

'Less of the old,' said Stomper. 'You're hardly a spring chicken, Trundler. More like an old turkey.'

I broke in. 'Stop it! The meteorite's gone!'

Stomper took off his cap and scratched his head. 'What d'you mean? How can it have "gone"? Where's it "gone" to?'

'I wonder ...' put in Trundler. 'Yesterday afternoon, as we were going out, Stomp, remember that helicopter ...?'

'Go on!' I cried.

'I'm just reflecting on whether it might have been able—?'

'Reflect in the car,' said Stomper. 'It's time we were off. Come on, Sam.'

* * *

The city was still half asleep at six o'clock in the morning.

Droplets of rain splashed the windscreen, and far away, over the rooftops, the sky kept blinking with lightning.

'Storm on the way,' said Stomper, switching on the radio in hope of a weather report, but instead it was news-time again.

'A spokesman for Squeaky Clean Music has offered a large reward for information leading to the arrest of Tony Tondi, the so called "Ice

Cream Man".

'Meanwhile, the hotel's owner, Mr Bernie Karbunkle, the ice cream millionaire, has pledged that BK Ice Creams will pay the ransom demand, on behalf of all decent ice cream men to set Michael Angelo free!

'As for the manager, Audrey Bapp, police are seeking to question her, following her disappearance from the hotel last night.'

'She's disappeared too?' exclaimed Trundler.

'So she's one of the gang!' I cried. 'Of course!'

It was obvious, really. Why hadn't I guessed before? Who else could have known Michael Angelo would visit Dad down in the cellar?

'Don't jump to conclusions,' said Stomper. 'Reflect on it, Trundler.'

'I will.' Trundler pulled into a side street. 'But first, find the manhole cover. Should be somewhere round here. Ready, Stomp?'

Stomper soon found the cover, and Trundler helped him to lift it.

And as the rain came down, bouncing back off the tarmac, I peered down into an oblong hole that was full of inky blackness.

'Go on, then,' said Trundler. 'Who's first?'

Chapter Eleven

I followed Stomper down, counting twelve iron rungs embedded in the brick shaft, before getting to the bottom.

'Good luck,' Trundler called. 'I'll be waiting.'

The cover fell back with a clang.

I shone my torch down the passage. The path was cobbled with slimy bricks, alongside a murky channel of slowly-moving brown water. The walls curved up and over, all furry with cobwebs and grime.

Stomper was probing the ground. 'Pity there aren't any footprints. The rogues can't have come this way.'

'So what do we do?' I said.

'Walk, Sam – to the Fright Hotel.'

The passage was far too narrow for Stomper to walk facing forwards, even by ducking his head. He had to take off his rucksack and shuffle along, going sideways, keeping his back to the wall.

My trainers squelched through the mud. I thought they were squeaking too, but when we both stopped for a moment, the squeaky noise carried on.

'Rats,' said Stomper. 'But look!'

He was pointing down at some footprints – heading in both directions.

I looked up, beaming my torch, and there was a rough sort of hole, blocked in with a rough wooden lid.

Stomper was grinning. 'Old Trundler was right!' He pushed at the lid with his stick. 'Won't seem to budge.'

'Might be boxes on top.' I remembered that gloomy storeroom lit by the iron lantern. 'That's why no one noticed it, Stomper, when they were searching the cellars.'

'That's it. Would you care for a sandwich?'

I couldn't feel hungry down here. The air wheezed out of the darkness like the bad breath of one of my teachers. And the squeaking was getting louder.

'That wind brings a warning,' said Stomper. 'The water's starting to rise and the rats don't want to get drowned.'

'Neither do I!' I said. 'Let's get moving.'

Both of us wanted to hurry, but the passages kept dividing. We had to keep checking for footprints.

And every time we moved on, the passage was narrower still, with even lower ceilings. Stomper's cap fell off and was swept away.

The puddles got wider and deeper as water lapped over the walkway.

Quite soon, all the footprints would be washed away, and what then?

'We're almost there, Sam.'

'Where?'

'Take a look at this map. There's a manhole up to South Street. I reckon the gang might have used that.'

A rat swam between his ankles, its eyes flashing yellow and green.

'Let's hope so.' I was shivering. Not that I cared about rats any more. What terrified me was the noise echoing down the tunnel like a train getting steadily closer.

The water was coming in waves now, splashing up over my knees. How far would we have to wade? The current was stronger. If it washed us away – end of story. A horrible slimy end.

Then who would save poor Dad? Nobody could, except Trundler – and he wouldn't have a clue that anything had gone wrong until …

I traced my fingertips over the wall. There were scratch marks. I stopped.

'Hurry up!' called Stomper.

'No, wait!' My torch beam flickered feebly, but when I shone it upwards it showed a square empty space where bricks had been cut from the ceiling, closed with a metal plate.

Stomper dropped his rucksack. As it went bobbing off downstream he raised his stick and pushed hard up, but the metal plate wouldn't budge, so I had to lend a hand too, and this time the plate slid away with a clang, dumping dust in our faces.

'Quick!' Stomper went down on one knee, clasping his hands together. 'Climb up on my back. Through the hole!'

Chapter Twelve

I came down with a thump, on all fours. I was inside an oblong pit.

Up above was a ramp with a car on. And over the rim of the pit, I picked out the ghostly shapes of three other big, smart cars, gleaming in the dim light.

'Oy, give us a hand!' called Stomper.

I pulled with all my might, one foot either side of the hole in the floor, both hands gripping Stomper's collar. Somehow, he heaved himself up, then rolled over, puffing for breath. 'So where ... d'you think ... we are?'

'It's an underground garage,' I said.

'The question is,' gasped Stomper, 'under what?'

A ramp led up to the exit at the far end of the garage. It was blocked by a heavy shutter, but a small door beside it opened on to a stairwell.

At the top was another doorway letting us into a hall with a marble floor and glass entrance. To the right was a porter's desk.

'So where's the porter?' said Stomper.

The porter was flat on the floor, hidden

behind his desk, alongside an overturned cup and a puddle of cold brown coffee.

'Spiked coffee, I bet you,' said Stomper, trying on the porter's blue cap.

'But where did the gang go from here?'

We both looked across to the entrance, just as a large, bulky woman pushed through the entrance doors. I'd barely glimpsed who it was when Stomper pulled me down, behind the porter's desk.

Audrey Bapp walked straight past the desk, to the far end of the hall where there was an elevator with buttons to press and steel doors.

We heard them hiss open and close and watched as the lights on the buttons went on, one by one, up and up to the top. We stared at each other.

'Wow!' I gasped. 'What's she up to?'

'She's one of the gang,' agreed Stomper.

Without even talking about it, we knew we were going up, too.

There were thirty-four little buttons, one for each of the floors; but only one was lit up now, and this was for thirty-four. We pressed the button marked 'Call'.

The lift began to descend. The doors slid open again, and in rather less than a minute we were on floor thirty-four. We stepped out into a lobby.

Ahead of us was a big sign.

Welcome to Bernie Karbunkle's Wonderful World of Ice Cream

'Well, I'll be blowed!' exclaimed Stomper.

'I don't understand this,' I said.

There was nobody in the office except one girl in green overalls who was mopping the floor.

'Has anyone else been here?' Stomper asked.

She shook her head. 'Not since Friday.'

'But someone came up to the top,' I said. 'Just a moment ago. We saw her!'

'This isn't the top. Top's the penthouse.'

'What penthouse?'

She pointed upwards. 'Belongs to Mr Karbunkle. Except he's not there at the moment.'

'But I never saw any button for a floor thirty-five,' grumbled Stomper.

'Of course not. Aren't you the porter?'

Stomper adjusted his cap.

'In that case,' added the cleaner, 'you must know there isn't a button! You just need your special pass key.'

'That's it.' He adjusted his cap once again. 'Silly me – must have left it downstairs. I'll just go and check on the fire doors.'

And off we went, crossing the office towards the emergency exit.

The fire escape staircase was hard and grey, zig-zagging down and down. But there were no stairs to the thirty-fifth floor. You'd never have guessed it existed.

I moved across to the window and gave the lever a tug. A platform for window-cleaning was swaying from ropes outside.

'Don't even consider it,' Stomper growled.

But I'd made up my mind already.

Chapter Thirteen

Grasping some safety rails, I caught a sick-making view down all those thirty-four storeys to a street with tiny cars that looked like matchbox toys. I tried to look up instead. The canopy billowed about, hiding much of the view, but even the sky looked dangerous, with mountains of shadowy clouds and shafts of yellow light beaming between the peaks.

Then Stomper heaved in behind me.

I tugged the nearest rope, making the platform lurch upwards on the left-hand side. Stomper pulled at the other end, setting it level, so I gave mine an extra tug, tilting it up again.

It was like going up on a see-saw – hundreds of feet from the ground.

We nearly tipped out more than once.

'You good at climbing ropes?' Stomper asked.

I laughed but it wasn't a joke. And when I caught sight of my grim white face reflected from a window on the thirty-fourth floor, all my confidence drained away.

I had tried a few climbing classes but …

'Wh-wh-why?' I stammered.

Stomper unthreaded some cords holding the canvas canopy on to its metal frame. Water splashed over his grizzled old head and plopped in big drips from his nose. Then the wind blew the canopy clean off its frame and it flapped away like a bird.

'Look up, look up,' called Stomper.

The pulleys holding the ropes were fixed to some big steel brackets sticking out from the edge of the roof, along with black metal casements, containing electric motors.

'No way am I climbing up there!'

'I'll give you a leg up,' said Stomper. 'And then I'll try to join you – but if I don't make it, keep going.'

'Wh-wh-where?'

'Find your Dad, Sam.'

I managed to raise one leg. I placed one trembling foot in between Stomper's clasped hands. And while I was telling myself this couldn't be all that different from getting out of the sewer into the underground car park, Stomper straightened up, giving me such a heave I went shooting up in the air – into the cloudy sky!

Somehow I grabbed the rope. I hung on, feet kicking empty air until I could get my knees round, then started to pull myself upwards, the rope tight between my legs.

At last one hand touched the pulley. My fingers closed over the top. Sliding my other hand inwards along the supporting strut, I swung out, letting it take my weight. My shins bashed into concrete.

Quickly I pulled my knees up over the parapet, twisting over sideways, only letting go of the strut when my feet were on solid ground. Then I grabbed at the iron railings, panting for breath. I'd made it!

But as I stood on that cold, narrow ledge I heard a loud whirring sound, then a harsh jangling noise. And when I looked over the edge, the platform was sliding away, with Stomper on board, waving feebly, unable to put on the brakes.

It was already halfway down before I caught sight of two figures, waiting on the pavement, with buckets and mops. Window cleaners?

They'd get a shock meeting Stomper.

But what about *me*? I was stuck up here – on the roof of a tower block, without any way to get down.

The wind was gale force now, blasting the building with rain, sweeping a huge wall of black cloud steadily closer and closer.

I guessed it would soon shroud the rooftop. As for what I could see of the roof, it was amazing, *un*real! A garden up in the sky. And bang in its midst, a giant white dome with a flat metal deck on its top. A helicopter was parked on this deck, looking like a fat pigeon roosting on a small nest.

I staggered past bushes and flowerpots, right up to the side of the dome, then carried on walking round it until I came to a door.

As I twisted the handle there was a flash and a monstrous crash of thunder.

Inside it was calm and quiet, with a round swimming pool in the middle, lined with glossy pink tiles. On the far side were three loungers, a couple of purple sun shades, even a bright yellow hammock strung between two palm trees. And also, what looked like a monster-sized ball, as tall as the meteorite, draped in a pink plastic sheet.

What else could it be? I was wondering, remembering that helicopter up on its pad overhead, when I heard voices below.

I stopped. Looking round, I noticed a steep metal spiral staircase, leading down to what I guessed was Karbunkle's penthouse. The walls were painted with murals of clowns and acrobats.

I went down the first few steps. On my left was a niche in the wall. A figure was crouching in it, shrouded in a black cloak. The hood slipped back from its head revealing a grinning skull, and its jaw dropped open.

'G-g-good morning!'

I staggered back, banging my elbow. I took a deep breath. I felt stupid. I knew it was only mechanical – something I'd brought it to life by putting my foot on a stair. Karbunkle's idea of a joke? But what if someone had heard it?

At the base of the stairs was a lobby, with a

doorway with rubberised seals. I pushed and the seals plopped apart, revealing a corridor.

Now I could hear the voices, more loudly and more clearly, but nobody seemed to have heard me.

So, holding my breath, I crept closer, feet padding along the mauve carpet. My heart was thumping so hard it felt as if it was trying to scramble out of my throat. I stopped by an open doorway.

The voices came from within.

And one of them was familiar because the voice belonged to ... my mum!

'My husband has crazy ideas,' she said, 'but he'd never do something like this.'

'You might not want to believe it,' responded a fake friendly voice, 'but your husband has kidnapped a pop star!'

'It doesn't make sense. He was with my son!'

'And what about Sam? Where is he?'

Me?

'If only I knew that. Wherever he is – if he's listening – please ... I ... I want you to phone me. I'm not cross at all, I just love you.'

I peered round the edge of the doorframe, in time to see Mum's anxious face, double its normal size, staring out from a giant TV screen – into an empty room.

Then the picture switched to a newsman

raising his hand to his earplug.

'I'm getting a message right now. We seem to have your husband live on the phone, so we'll cut to …'

A photo of Dad – quite an old one – in front of his ice cream parlour. And then Dad's voice, faint and crackly.

'This is the Ice Cream Man. Michael Angelo is happy and well, he's eating my Moonmallow Smoothie. But make sure I get my money. I want it left in the waste skip behind the Fright Hotel. By midnight, or else. If you try any tricks Mike pays – with his life! Up to you.'

'You know who that was?' said the news man.

'That's him,' gulped Mum. 'Sam's father.'

Chapter Fourteen

I knew Dad had his faults, but he wasn't a crook
– or a monster. And yet I had heard his voice.

Groping about for a lamp switch I ended up
tugging the blind. It went shooting up with a
twang. But all I could see outside was a thick
grey wall of blankness pressing against the glass.

I turned off the TV.

What could have happened to Stomper? Was
he waiting down in the street? Perhaps he had
phoned the police? Though what could Stomper
have told them? Only that I was up here. That
was my choice. Would they care? Then I
remembered Audrey Bapp coming up here in
the lift. All I could do was keep looking.

With Dad's crazy tee-hee voice still echoing
round my brain, I padded on down the corridor,
checking in all the rooms.

I found myself in a study with bookshelves
and black leather chairs and one wall lined with
certificates mounted in silver frames …

> **First Prize for Vanilla Ice Cream**
> **Awarded to: Bernard Karbunkle**

Karbunkle had won lots of prizes. I couldn't imagine why. His ice creams were cheap, mass-produced – nothing like Dad's home-made ones, let alone Moonmallow Smoothie.

But then I noticed the small print, down on the bottom line …

Awarded every year by the Karbunkle Foundation

Ha!

I turned on my heel, only to come face to face with a portrait on the wall of a plump man with a crown on his head, wearing scarlet robes. He was holding a regal sceptre that looked like a golden cornet topped with a pile of ice cream. And down in the bottom right corner, enscribed on a painted scroll, I read …

The Kornet King
Bernard Karbunkle the First

I didn't know what to think. This was like an extraordinary dream.

I carried on down the corridor, and came to the penthouse kitchen.

A table was laid for breakfast, with two plates and bowls, rolls and jam, but there was no one there, either. I went on through an archway, into a grand sort of loft space, with plate glass windows on two sides, huge sofas and free-standing lamps, and another door at the end, with a phone on the wall beside it. I wondered about calling Mum, but as I tiptoed towards the phone, I heard a familiar voice – so loud, so clear, so *breathy* – no way was it on TV.

'Lucky old Ice Cream Man! You'd never have done it without me.'

It was Audrey Bapp. She was in there!

'You've scared 'em all – even your wife.'

But who was she talking to? Not my dad?

'Tee-hee! I'm ever so grateful. I'll be more famous than Bernie, I'll be the new Kornet King!'

I felt really wobbly and sick. But somehow, with three careful paces, I made it to the doorway. In front of me was a small empty room with sliding mirror doors hiding built-in wardrobes. The voices came from the next room.

But before I could see who was in there I heard Audrey again, her voice going extra deep.

'I'm gonna change out of my clobber.'

Clobber? I stopped in my tracks. Clobber meant clothes – it meant wardrobes. It meant I needed to hide!

Squeezing between two sliding doors, I burrowed between the racks of clothes dangling from rows of hangers, turning to make a small peep-hole as Audrey came out of the bedroom.

She was wearing the same mauve scarf, the same white housecoat and tights. I gawped as she undid her housecoat.

Underneath there were straps and supports for holding her big soft bosoms. Or that's what I thought they were for. Until she reached round behind her back in order to undo the clasps, and two pink squelchy balloon things plopped off on to the floor.

And then Audrey took off 'her' wig.

Chapter Fifteen

I was so stunned and staggered I simply buried my face in the folds of a bold check jacket to stop myself yelling out loud. But Bapp's plump hands reached in on either side of my head, so I had to lurch out of range as the jacket was pulled from its hanger. He was putting on Karbunkle's clothes.

The doors slid shut with a click.

I couldn't get out with those doors locked. I nearly shouted for help, but any help I got from Bapp would land me in more trouble. Audrey Bapp was my enemy – whoever he really was.

I heard him walk away. I heard a door slam. Nothing else. No other mad comments from Dad, so Dad must have gone as well.

Though if that had really been Dad, it had to mean one of two things. Either my dad was mad, or else, what was he? A crook – a villain, an evil monster who was threatening to murder a pop star?

Rubbish!

But it wasn't rubbish. I'd seen the news on

TV and heard Mum agree, 'It's my husband.' I didn't know what to believe.

My eyes began to adjust. There was just enough light seeping through to read the time on my watch. I read it again, and again, and noticed the time moving on.

And even though I was in such a mess, my tummy started to rumble.

Wonderful – perfect timing! I'd not had a bite of those sandwiches Stomper had brought in his rucksack, not even helped myself from Bernie Karbunkle's kitchen, yet now I was locked in this wardrobe I felt incredibly hungry.

I had to get out.

I tried. I tried everything I could think of – like rattling and joggling the doors, and trying to force them apart, and thumping at the back wall.

I even tried hauling myself up over the hanging rail, arching my back in an effort to force my way up through the ceiling – but this was no cheap wardrobe. The ceiling was solid concrete. So all I managed to do was get myself hot and sticky, and even more hungry and thirsty and also … desperately tired.

I slumped on a soft heap of clothes.

There were still nearly twelve hours to go before the deadline expired. Twelve hours to get out of this wardrobe.

I let my thoughts wander a bit, remembering Mum on the telly, appealing for me to make contact, saying, 'I'm worried about him.'

Dear Mum. I wished that I'd phoned her. But thinking that didn't do any good.

My thoughts began to drift. I remembered the day when the drill broke, and Mum decided to leave. And long before that, I remembered the nights when I had lain awake hearing Mum and Dad quarrelling about the ice cream parlour, because it was losing them money, with Dad trying hard to persuade her that things were sure to get better, if he just got a small lucky break.

I squeezed my eyes tight and remembered wishing as hard as I could that something would come his way to make things go well for a change.

And *hah*! That meteorite had come bouncing into our lives, and what had it brought?

Chaos. Madness.

* * *

The next time I opened my eyes I knew I had been asleep, if only because I'd been dreaming that I was back in the sewers. Not a good dream. I'd been drowning, trying to keep afloat by holding on to the tail of an enormous black rat, while Dad paddled by on a lilo, calling over his shoulder: 'I'm off to the Fright Hotel, Sam, to pick up the loot – see you later!'

My watch said ten past eleven. Odd, unless it had stopped and gone back into reverse, or else I must have been sleeping for eight, nine … how many hours?

Dad's deadline was less than an hour off!

I rummaged about, banged the door, and tried to balance myself by stretching my arms either side. One hand went through a wide, narrow slit in the wall that I hadn't noticed before, into a soft, woolly space.

My fingers explored up and down. There were five other drawers, all supported on thin metal  runners, from shoulder height down to the floor.

I shunted the middle drawer out. It made a dull thud on the carpet, spilling out tartan socks.

The next drawer was packed with boxer shorts covered with Mickey Mouse pictures. The third was full of bow ties. And once I'd pushed out the rest of the drawers I just had to work at the runners until they came loose in my hands. Then I could squeeze through the hole!

Lights blazed in every room, but all I could hear was a gentle buzz from the refrigerator, and the distant howling of wind beyond the plate glass windows. I had the whole place to myself.

I found the phone and dialled Barry's number, trying to call Mum, but all I got was the answerphone. I left a hasty message. 'I'm up in the Karbunkle Tower, Mum!'

My legs were as stiff as old logs. Pins and needles were fizzing away from my knees to the tips of my toes, so when I got up to the study I sat on a black leather chair, intending to think about things. Instead, I noticed a dictaphone on Karbunkle's giant desk. I got up and switched it on.

At once I heard Audrey Bapp saying, 'Hello and welcome to the new Fright Hotel. How nice to see you. It's ever so nice.' And then 'she' repeated herself. And then I heard Dad again. 'This is the Ice Cream Man. Michael Angelo's happy and well ... Happy and well. No, that's not quite right.' But this sounded more like Audrey. Or could it be somebody else?

For a while, all these voices were chattering on and I found myself staring at that portrait of Bernie Karbunkle.

There was something about his chubby round face, something about those sharp eyes, something about those full fleshy lips curved up in a smug sort of grin. Something – but what?

Then I got it. He looked like 'Audrey Bapp'.

I needed more time to think about this. I switched off the dictaphone.

Had it been Bernie Karbunkle playing a part? Surely not.

Besides, why kidnap a pop star and ask for a massive ransom, then offer to pay it himself?

Not for Dad's benefit, surely?

* * *

I pushed through the doors to the lobby. Climbing those spiral stairs, I made sure I took a long stride to miss out the crucial step. The skull in the niche kept quiet.

I looked all around. Dark outside. The only light in the dome glowed up from the depths of the pool, tinting the steam on its surface a wispy candyfloss pink.

Passing the loungers and palm trees, I went up to the big round object draped in the plastic sheet. But before I could lift a corner and take a peep underneath I heard someone let out a groan.

It came from a door labelled 'Pump Room'. One twist and the door was open.

My fingers groped for the light switch. But as the strip-lights flickered over the machinery that made up the heating system, I heard another low groan. I looked up. Strung from the pipes that criss-crossed the concrete ceiling, I realised there was a body, squirming, caught in a web – with a blindfold wrapped round his eyes.

Chapter Sixteen

Dad was properly caught – bound up in a sticky black net that held him, feet off the ground, arms trapped tight by his sides.

I called to him and he answered. But I didn't know what to do.

'How did you—? When did you—? *Why*, Dad?'

'They left me here some time last night, Sam. They've got Michael Angelo, too.'

'They?'

'They were wearing masks, Sam. I haven't a clue who they are.'

'You promise you aren't their ... leader?'

Dad acted as if I was joking, but he was too tired to laugh. 'Just get me down, will you, please, Sam? And tell me, how did you find me?'

I told him my side of the story, but when I got to the bit about seeing Mum on TV, I broke off, staring at Dad.

'Your voice ...' I repeated. 'I heard you. Mum recognised your voice. But it was all wrong. It was mad, Dad.'

'I don't quite get what you're meaning ...'

But I did. Out of thin air. Though it was

obvious, really.

I had only heard Dad – or someone who sounded like Dad. I hadn't seen Dad from the wardrobe, because Dad hadn't been there.

I thought of those voices I'd listened to on the dictaphone in Bernie Karbunkle's study. Karbunkle must have been practising, not only to sound like 'Audrey' but also to mimic my dad. (That shouldn't have been too hard for him – even I could copy Dad's voice!) I was filled with a rush of excitement. I still had a dad I could trust!

But as I tried to undo the knot that was holding the blindfold in place, I heard a low, clattering noise getting steadily louder.

'The helicopter,' said Dad. 'They flew off and now they're returning!'

I tore at the net, but the ropes were too strong and the knots were far too tight.

The noise swelled into a shuddering roar. By now, it was overhead.

The helicopter was landing.

'Leave me,' cried Dad. 'You're our only hope. You can't let them find you. Hide!'

* * *

Shooting out of the pump room, I dived under that plastic sheet. My head bashed into hard rock. No doubt about what that was – though all I could see were stars! But no time to think about that now.

I squirmed along under the sheet and lifted one edge to peer out.

A loud buzzing, high in the air, made me look up. A panel was sliding open in the roof of the dome. A ladder began to slide down, unfolding section by section until its rubber-tipped feet bumped on to the pink tiled floor. Then a pair of brown boots appeared, worn over some baggy trousers, and *then* I caught sight of a big plump man, wearing that loud check jacket that 'Bapp' had put on this morning.

Close behind came a short twitchy man in a black leather flying suit, with a prickly moustache and big goggles perched on top of his head so he looked like an overblown fly. But where had I seen him before?

Of course! In the ice cream parlour! Yes, this was the 'health inspector'!

But who was behind him? Poor Stomper, his hands trussed behind his back, guarded by two men in overalls (the 'window-cleaners', no doubt).

I suddenly felt very scared.

The man in the loud check jacket glanced at his chunky gold watch.

'We haven't got long. Ten minutes and you must be off again, to the Fright Hotel to pick up my money. But first, we must fetch our "Ice Cream Man".'

The 'health inspector' saluted. 'Yes, Mr Karbunkle. Of course, sir.'

'Good. Have a look in the pump room!'

The 'window-cleaners' pushed Stomper towards the 'health inspector' and headed towards the doorway.

They came out, dragging Dad with the blindfold still round his face.

'Well, well.' Karbunkle acted suprised. 'I wonder who this could be?'

His men gave Dad a few pushes and cuffs, as if to get him to answer.

'Care-ful.' Karbunkle was soothing. 'I know I should phone the police, to tell them I've caught an intruder, but as I'm a fellow ice cream man,' – he sat himself down on a lounger, stretching his legs – 'let's consider. And take off his blindfold, please, boys.'

I watched Dad blink in the light.

'That's better.' Karbunkle was smiling. 'You *are* in a mess. The whole world thinks you've kidnapped a famous pop star – with my manager, Audrey Bapp. You all got away through a sewer and ended up here in my absence, so you could steal my 'copter. My pilot will vouch for this. He'll tell the police he was hi-jacked – made to to fly to the Fright Hotel to pick up the ransom money!'

'I'm innocent – and you know it,' cried Dad.

'You've framed me!'

'That's not how it looks, though. It looks like *you* tried to frame *me*!'

'It's been you all along,' Dad shouted. 'You sabotaged my Smoothie in my ice cream parlour, and then you sent in this rat' – Dad pointed at the pilot – 'Acting as a health inspector!'

'How true!' Karbunkle tittered. 'I fooled you, by being so clever, and now you're properly stitched. But I'm not nasty. I'll help you escape.'

Karbunkle took out a wallet. 'I'll give you a whole wad of money, false passport, first class ticket to a sunny place far away where you can start a new life.'

Dad shook his head. 'I'm not stupid.'

The palm trees rustled and shivered.

'Stupid? The choice is yours. Either you let me help you out, or else you go now, with my pilot. But once he's picked up the ransom he'll go and land on the golf course, then scoot off into the darkness, leaving you trapped on board – so he can call the police, and then you'll get caught with my money. You'll end up with ten years in gaol. And why should I care? That's the question. Because you've got something I want. One little thing.'

'What's that?' said Dad.

'I want your recipe, please.'

'You think I'd just tell you?' exclaimed Dad.

'After all this?'

'Not the first time. I did ask before. I asked nicely – straight after you were featured on *The Real Food Show*. I made you a really good offer. But you were so rude,' said Karbunkle.

'You're just a cheap trickster,' said Dad.

'And you're just a has-been ice cream man! You'll never make Moonmallow Smoothie, not ever again, because …' – his grin was triumphant – 'I'll show you. Pull off the sheet!'

The pink sheet was tugged from the meteorite.

I tried to squirm out of sight, but one of those men in overalls lunged at me, grabbing my sleeve.

'My goodness!' Karbunkle was beaming, his voice going up a whole octave so he sounded like Audrey again. 'Aren't I the lucky one, look what we've got. The meteorite *and* the boy, Dad's cute little helper. Hello, Sam!'

He pushed out two fat hands.

'Don't touch him,' Dad shouted. 'You leave him.'

'I'll let him go when you've told me.' He gripped my ears with both hands. 'Or I'm going to rip these off and feed 'em to Michael's poodles!'

'No, listen,' Dad stalled, 'There's a formula – but it'll take time to work out. I'll need a computer—'

'Don't play games with me. You've made it

before. Tell me *now*!'

But at that crucial moment I knew what I needed to do. My ears were throbbing.

'I'll help.'

Karbunkle let go of my ears.

'So what do you know?' he said. 'Spill it all out. Ingredients … chemicals … methods?'

'No, no, it's quite simple,' I said.

His eyes were all glinty and eager. 'Tell Bernie and you'll be rewarded. Ten times the pocket money you normally get in a year – or shall I say twenty times?' He looked round at Dad with a ludicrous smirk. 'Or shall we say thirty times a whole year's pocket money, all in one go? Win the jackpot, by being a sensible boy.'

'Tell your guard to let go, then I'll show you,' I said.

He nodded and I was set free. Then I walked round the meteorite until I was standing behind it, facing the pool. 'The thing is – it's what's in the middle,' I said. 'You mix it with water. Like this.'

And that's when I gave it a push.

* * *

It rolled slowly over the pink tiles towards the edge of the pool. It teetered, tilting back from the rim. So I heaved it and over it went, with an enormous splash.

The noise echoed all round the dome.

Karbunkle just stood with his hands in the air,

86

gawping in amazement as a thin streak of foam bilged out. It spewed slowly up from the drill-hole in the side of the meteorite. Up over the side of the pool, hitting the health inspector full in the face! Down he went.

Karbunkle just stood there in horrified shock as the meteorite tilted slightly, sending the foam jetting upwards, forming a frothy white fountain, gushing higher and higher until it was splashing the ceiling.

The pool was soon buried in foam.

And as the foam mounted up, wodging and woggling out of the pool, I caught sight of Bernie Karbunkle holding out his hands as if to stop the stuff – but the Moonmallow foam rolled over him in an unstoppable wave.

'Get up the ladder,' Dad shouted, making a grab for Stomper.

Karbunkle's men tried to stop us, but Dad was far too quick, tripping one of them over and giving the other a push. Then Dad was hauling Stomper as fast as he could up the ladder, and I was scrambling behind them.

Karbunkle came behind me. He nearly grabbed hold of one ankle but somehow I kicked myself free, and made it, on to the deck.

The wind nearly lifted me off.

'Look out, Sam, behind you!' cried Stomper.

Karbunkle pushed me aside. He lunged at Stomper. Stomper fell back, and Karbunkle waddled away, throwing himself through the open hatch, into the helicopter. His pilot, the 'health inspector', jumped in close behind him, slamming the hatch in Dad's face.

I heard a loud clattering roar. I guessed they were going to escape, but the blades didn't move. What was happening?

Then Stomper was tugging my sleeve, shouting into my ear, pointing up in the air – at another helicopter hovering over the deck.

Floodlamps cut the darkness.

And shielding my eyes from the glare, I heard a voice boom out through a megaphone, *'Police – police – Put your hands up!'*

Chapter Seventeen

It was all over in no time.

Policemen in combat gear abseiled down to the deck, then the helicopter came in to land on the lawn beside the dome.

I heard a familiar voice.

'Ah there you are, Sammy, old feller. Still in top form. That's the spirit!'

'Trundler!' I cried. 'How d'you get here?'

'Why, with my old police chums – on this 'copter, of course.'

'But how did you guess where to find us?'

'Me – *guess*?' Trundler's chin went all saggy. 'I had to do some reflecting, then did some investigating. Got a few leads. Made deductions.'

'Oh, cut out the hogwash,' said Stomper.

So Trundler explained things more clearly.

After saying farewell at the manhole he had taken some time for reflecting – about Audrey Bapp.

'Didn't get far, until I happened to notice a photograph on the wall, Stomp, from one of our old pantomimes. Made me ponder a moment on what Sam had said about Bapp. "Like me, as a pantomime dame." And somehow that made me sit up.'

'Please, stick to the point,' Stomper growled.

'But this *is* the point. The whole point, old Stomp. Because when I looked through my albums of pantos we did years ago – I came across the Cheshire Cat from *Alice in Wonderland*!'

'For crying out loud!' exclaimed Stomper.

But Trundler was looking quite stern. 'No, who do you think played the cat? I'll give you a clue. Not Audrey!'

Stomper was scrubbing his bristles.

'Bernie Karbunkle?' I said.

Trundler gave me a look that went from solemn and puzzled through to a satisfied grin. 'How did you work that out?'

'Sheer genius?' muttered Stomper.

'It didn't make sense,' said Trundler. 'Not till I tried to find Bapp, and nobody knew where she'd come from, let alone where she'd gone! So then I sat up even straighter and put on my thinking cap, and thought about who was left. Who had the best alibi? It was Bernie Karbunkle, of course, because he'd been "out of the country", and if he was paying the ransom no one was going to suspect him. But when I reflected, I realised he had some very good reasons for wanting to frame Sam's dad.'

'To stop me being a rival,' said Dad. 'And force the recipe from me.'

'But no one believed me,' said Trundler. 'Not even my old police pals. Not until Sam's mum gave them a call, saying Sammy had left a message from the top of the Karbunkle tower! And then they decided they'd better "check up, to check Mr K was OK!" So here we are. Just in time, Stomp!'

'Too late for the best bit,' said Stomper.

'What best bit?'

Stomper grinned. 'Sam gave "Mr K" a quick lesson in how to make Moonmallow Smoothie. And what's more, he gave him a dome full. More than he bargained for, eh, Sam?'

'What *do* you mean?' Trundler wondered.

I looked at Dad. He looked happy. Not like a man who had just lost the only stuff on the planet for making his Moonmallow Smoothie.

'I could have explained it,' said Dad. 'If he'd found me a pen and some paper.'

I stared at him. 'How do you mean, Dad?'

He woggled his eyebrows. 'Well, Sam, I've finally worked out the formula for getting that foamy reaction. I'd been trying to crack it for weeks, but there were so many distractions. Until last night, strung up in that net, it fell into place in my head.'

'What? Meteorite plus water, Dad?'

'Not with my formula, no. Just various bits and pieces I'll get from the hardware store, and plenty of natural products. Mind you, I must do some more tests.'

Chapter Eighteen

I didn't mention these 'tests' when I phoned Mum to tell her we were safe.

There was enough to explain, especially about Michael Angelo. 'Tell Zoe we found him, Mum!'

We had found him locked in a cabin, up on the helipad, still gorging on Moonmallow Smoothie and looking a little bit sickly.

As for Dad, when we got back home, he went straight into his 'lab' and stayed up all night doing 'tests' – as if the Karbunkle business had just been a minor distraction. I didn't see Dad again until the following morning when he tottered into the kitchen with a bucket full of white foam.

'This is home-made!'

'Not in here, Dad. I'm trying to clear this place up.'

Dad opened his mouth to protest, but the front doorbell buzzed. 'Who could that be?'

Both of us raced to the door.

A white stretch limo was out in the street, and two enormous white poodles were bouncing around on the doorstep, along with the famous pop star who was wearing a white silk suit.

He came in and looked round the garden, saw the hole where the pond had once been and told us the night in the cabin, on top of the Karbunkle Tower, had been the best night of his life – all thanks to the Moonmallow Smoothie.

'I managed to eat the whole lot, as well as that sticky spongy base with those yummy squashy green bits in. Now I need more, loads more Smoothie!'

He needed it for himself, and all his musicians and crew, to keep them happy on tour. 'And we could have Moonmallow Smoothie stalls at all my gigs, for the fans!'

Dad and I looked at each other.

'I'm sorry,' said Dad. 'Love to help but ... I don't think I can, to be honest.'

I looked in Dad's bucket. 'Why not?'

'I'd need to have somewhere to make it.'

'Well, buy somewhere,' Michael said softly.

'Come again?'

Michael just rolled on. 'I mean, you'll get the reward – from Squeaky Clean Music – you earned it. And I'm gonna double it, too, to make it a personal thank you. You're gonna be rolling in dosh, man!'

Dad took a deep breath. 'Well, in that case ... I suppose I could buy a small factory. If Sam's in agreement?'

'Of course, Dad!'

'OK, it's a deal!'

They shook hands.

And suddenly there was clapping from over the garden wall, and Stomper and Trundler leant over, with plates of pizzas and buns, so Dad invited them round too, to join in the celebrations.

Then Dad had to telephone Mum. He asked her if she'd come home, please?

She asked if the rock was still there.

He said it had been 'taken care of'.

So Mum is on her way home now ... and everything's going to be fine.

Other titles available in Black Cats ...

Great stories for hungry readers